THE Deep and Snowy Wood

Elwyn
Tate

In the deep
and snowy wood
where the cold
winds BLOW,

one deer runs

leaving tracks in the snow.

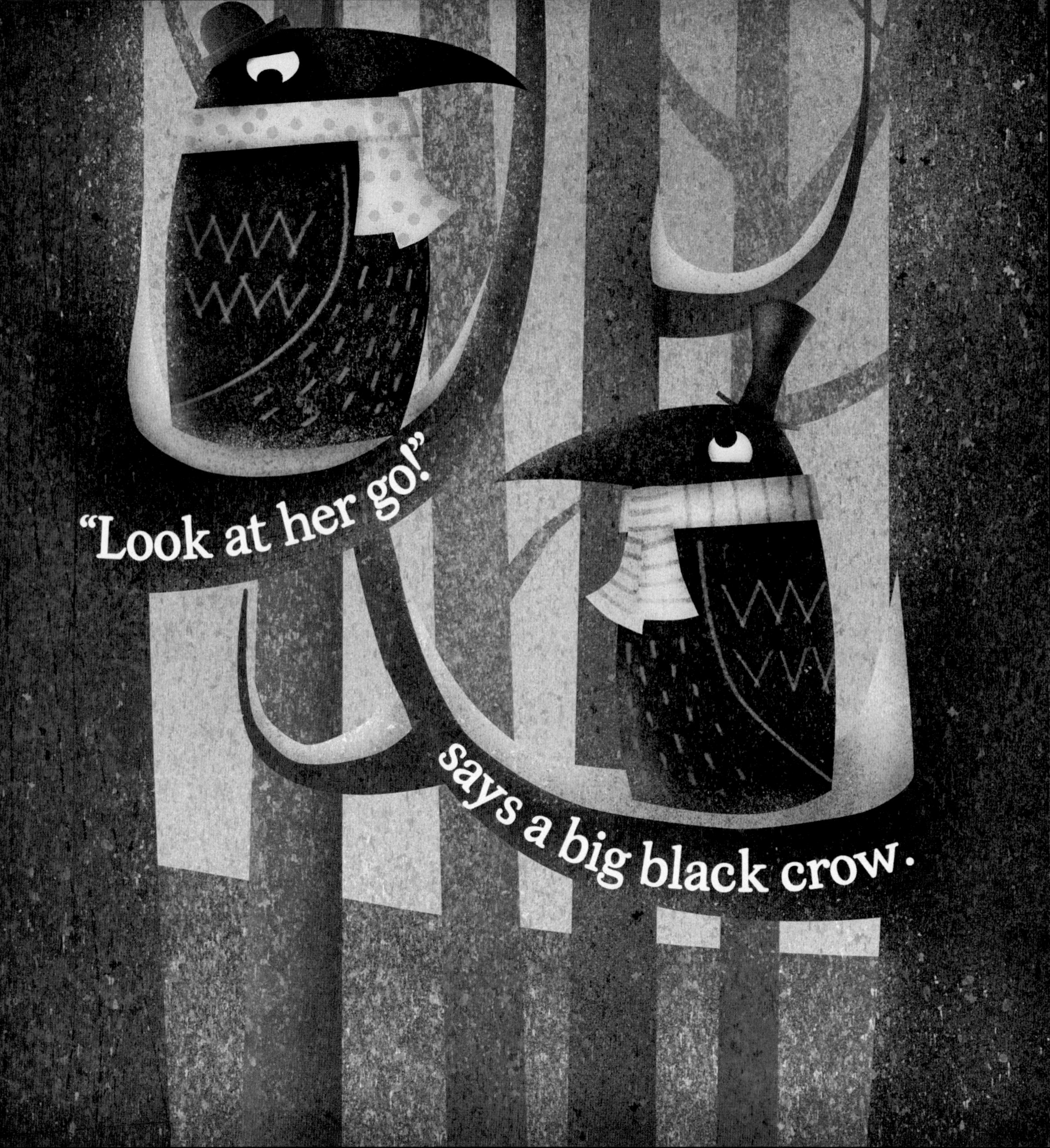

"Look at her go!" says a big black crow.

But where is she going?

The crows don't know.

In the deep snowy wood

where a tree lies flat,

One squirrel hops past a badger...

Hop!

and a bat.

In the deep and snowy wood

where the hills dip and roll,

one mole digs in an underground hole.

He digs past a vole

and a duck on a stroll.

But where will he dig...

in his underground hole?

Run,

run,

run.

Dig,

dig,

dig.

Hop, hop,

hop.

they ...   ...stop?

A deer, a squirrel and
a mole in the snow.

Why are they
waiting?
What do they know?

In the deep and
snowy wood
so far far away,

from over the hills
comes the sound
of a sleigh.

Jingle jingle!
Jingle jingle!

The animals cheer,
"Hooray! Hooray!"
And now EVERYONE
knows...

...it's Christmas day!

Merry
Christmas.